# DISNEY · PIXAR

# TALES TO FINISH
## COLOR YOUR OWN STORYBOOK COLLECTION!

**Disney** PRESS

Los Angeles • New York

All illustrations by the Disney Storybook Art Team

Published by Disney Press, an imprint of Disney Book Group. No part of this book may be reproduced or transmitted in any form or by any means, electronic or mechanical, including photocopying, recording, or by any information storage and retrieval system, without written permission from the publisher. For information address Disney Press, 1101 Flower Street, Glendale, California 91201.

Printed in the United States of America

First Hardcover Edition, May 2017

1 3 5 7 9 10 8 6 4 2

FAC-008598-17097

ISBN 978-1-4847-9942-0

Library of Congress Control Number: 2016948964

For more Disney Press fun, visit www.disneybooks.com

**Logo Applies to Text Stock Only**

# CONTENTS

# Disney · PIXAR

# TALES to FINISH

Follow your favorite Disney • Pixar characters on seven exciting adventures! Color in the art on every page, add the missing characters to the scene, and create your own endings to every story to finish these Pixar tales your own way!

**W**oody the cowboy doll stood at the window in Andy's bedroom. He watched as Andy stepped onto the bus, and the bus quickly pulled away. Then he turned around and looked at the other toys. "All clear!" he announced. "Andy's off to school."

The toys gathered on the floor in the middle of the room, surrounding a long cardboard box. Andy had brought it home the night before. Woody climbed down from the desk and walked over to the box. "Now," he said, "let's get a look at whatever this is."

Woody flipped open the box flaps and looked inside. He saw several rubber tubes and a tall plastic stand. It was a rocket launcher!

"How far do you think it goes?" Rex the dinosaur asked.

"There's only one way to find out," Buzz Lightyear the space ranger replied. He started to lift pieces out of the box.

Woody helped Buzz put the rocket together. When it was finished, Buzz said, "Now, who wants to go first?"

"I do!" Jessie the cowgirl said as she jumped up and raised her hand.

Buzz showed her what to do. There was a pump attached to the launch pad. Jessie stepped on the pump as hard as she could, and the rocket shot up into the air. It floated for a minute before landing lightly on Andy's desk.

"Cool," said Hamm the piggy bank. "Can I try?"

"Sure, everyone can try," Woody said. He climbed up onto the desk and pushed the rocket off.

When it was all set up again, Hamm stomped on the pump. *Whoosh!* The rocket shot all the way across the room.

Buzz and Woody helped set up the rocket for each toy and then measured the distance that the rocket flew with the string from a yo-yo.

"Looks like we have a tie," said Buzz after all the toys had taken a turn.

"Yep," Woody agreed. "Hamm and Slink both made it all the way to Andy's door."

"We need a tiebreaker!" Jessie said.

"That's a great idea," Woody replied. He helped Buzz set up the rocket, and then they turned to face the other toys.

"We could do one final stomp," Buzz suggested. "That puts the pressure on Slink and Hamm."

Slinky Dog and Hamm both agreed.

Woody held his hands behind his back. Slinky Dog and Hamm had to guess how many fingers he was holding up to see who would go first. Slinky picked five and Hamm guessed three.

"Five is right! Slinky goes first," Woody said, holding up his wide-open hand.

Slinky Dog walked over to the rocket. He stretched his body and rolled his head from side to side to loosen up. When he was ready, he nodded to Buzz.

"Okay," Buzz announced to all the toys. "This is it, the big stomp. Slinky and Hamm will each try to launch the rocket as far as he can by stomping on the pump. They only get one try. Whoever makes the rocket fly farther is the winner."

The other toys fell silent as they watched Slinky Dog step up to the pump. Slinky lifted his front paw. *"Grr,"* he growled as he pushed down on the pump as hard as he could. But the rocket didn't move!

Slinky Dog looked at the rocket sitting on its stand. "What happened?" he asked.

"I don't know, Slink," Buzz said as he walked around the rocket. "It looks like it's all set up correctly."

Hamm walked up to the rocket as Slinky Dog backed away. "I'll give it a try," he said.

He counted to three and then stomped his foot on the pump. But the rocket still didn't move.

**ADD THE MISSING ALIEN!**

"What do you think happened?" Woody asked Buzz.

Buzz smiled. "I think we have some space invaders," he said. He opened a small door on the rocket.

The three Little Green Aliens peered out at everyone.

"Hey, guys," Woody said. "What are you doing in there?"

"Go to Earth," the aliens said together. One of them pointed toward the corner of the room by Andy's desk.

Woody looked at Buzz, confused. Buzz looked over at the desk and saw a globe sitting on top. Andy had been using it the night before for a school project.

Buzz helped the aliens climb out of the rocket. "Sorry, guys," he said. "You're already on Earth. That is just a tiny scale model of the real—"

"Um, Buzz," Woody interrupted. He knew Buzz could ramble on about the galaxy for hours. "Can we get back to the contest? Slink and Hamm want to see who can shoot this rocket to the moon!"

The other toys clapped and cheered, ready to get the contest back underway. Slinky Dog stretched again as he waited for Buzz to give him the all-clear. Then he stepped up to the pump.

Slinky Dog stomped on the pump as hard as he could. The rocket shot off the stand and flew across the room.

"Oooh," the Little Green Aliens said as they watched it fly.

"Good job, Slink!" Woody said.

"That'll be a tough one to beat," Rex said.  He waited by the rocket while Woody measured the distance with the string.

Hamm stepped up for his turn. Rex was waiting across the room where Slinky Dog's rocket had landed to show Hamm how far his had to go. Hamm stomped on the pump and his rocket shot into the air. Everyone held their breath as they watched it fly. Then it landed . . . in the same place Slinky Dog's had!

"Another tie!" Jessie yelled. "What do we do now?"

Slinky Dog looked at Hamm. Hamm looked at Slinky Dog.

"What if we give the aliens a ride?" Hamm suggested.

"That's a great idea!" Woody exclaimed as the aliens cheered.

"Ride into space," they said as they shuffled back over to the launching pad.

"You'll have to go one at a time," Buzz said as he helped the first alien into the rocket. He stuck a handkerchief into the small space around the alien. "Can't hurt to have some extra cushioning," he said.

For the rest of the morning, the aliens rode one at a time in the rocket. Each of the toys took a turn stomping on the pump to see how far they could make the aliens fly.

When the other toys got tired of playing with the rocket, Buzz and the aliens sat beside the globe.

"Well, fellas," Buzz said, "what did you think about your rocket ride?"

"Fun," they said. "Tomorrow we go home."

"You are home, guys," he said.

ADD BUZZ TO THE SCENE!

"How are our space invaders doing?" Woody asked. "Slink and Hamm were just saying that they think if they worked together they could launch all three of you in one go."

## HOW DOES THE STORY END? WRITE YOUR OWN ENDING.

_____

_____

_____

_____

_____

# ICE RACERS

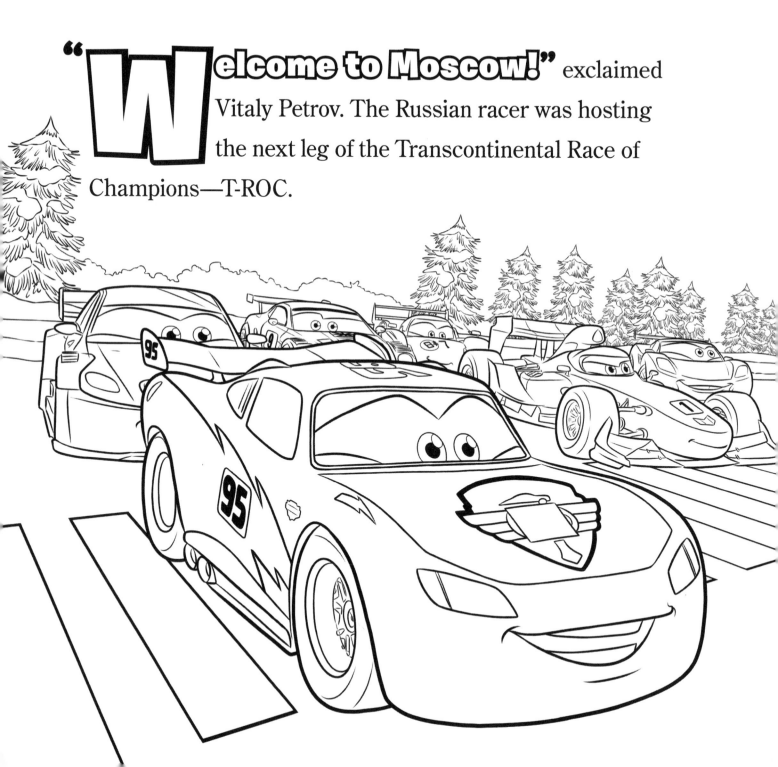

"**Welcome to Moscow!**" exclaimed Vitaly Petrov. The Russian racer was hosting the next leg of the Transcontinental Race of Champions—T-ROC.

"Moscow is amazing, Vitaly!" said Lightning McQueen.

"If you think the city is beautiful,
wait until you see the countryside,"
Vitaly said. "We'll be ice racing
there tomorrow."

COLOR IN THE MAP!

The next morning, the racers gathered in Vitaly's

headquarters. A major snowstorm had passed through Moscow

overnight. It was all anyone could talk about!

Carla Veloso, the racer from Brazil, peered out a window.

"There's nearly a meter of snow on the ground!" she said.

"That's in the city," added Lightning. "The conditions will be even worse in the countryside."

"Don't worry, everyone. I will find a solution!" said Vitaly.

Vitaly quickly plotted a new race course through the city. "We can race on the closed roads with studded tires," he said.

Soon the racers were ready to go. They pulled up to the starting line at Saint Battery's Cathedral.

"Is everyone ready to ice race?" Vitaly called out.

The racers answered by revving their engines.

"Let's put these tires to the test!" Lightning yelled.

The racers zoomed away, leaving a cloud of snow behind them.

Soon the racers passed the historic Balljoint Theater. "The most beautiful ballet and opera performances in the world are held at the Balljoint," Vitaly called back to his friends.

Shu Todoroki, the Japanese racer, couldn't help smiling at the Russian racer. "Not only does he make this look easy, he's giving us a tour at the same time."

Just as the racers completed the first circle around the city, they encountered a roadblock. "It's no problem! Follow me!" Vitaly shouted. He sped down a ramp and into an underground metro station. The racers admired the graceful archways and the marble floors. But most of all, they appreciated the warmth!

As the racers emerged from the station, they were caught off guard by a truck carrying huge bales of hay. The hay was covering the truck's eyes, so he couldn't see the oncoming racers!

Vitaly, Raoul ÇaRoule, Lightning, Francesco Bernoulli, and Max Schnell quickly swerved around the truck. But Rip Clutchgoneski couldn't make it. He turned too quickly and spun out!

Vitaly looked back to make sure Rip was okay.

"I'm fine!" Rip yelled out to his friends as he came to a stop on the side of the road. "Don't worry, I'll catch up!"

When the racers reached the bank of the frozen Moscow
River, Vitaly presented them with an option. "Since there might
be more hazards on the road ahead, you may want to take a
detour along the river."

Some of the racers looked concerned.

"The choice is yours," Vitaly said.

Five of the racers decided to stick to the road, while the other seven decided to take the river route. They would all meet up at the Central Moscow Hybridrome, where they would complete three laps before crossing the finish line.

Vitaly gave the river racers a few words of advice. "Stay close to the bank, where the ice is more solid. If you are going too fast, ease off the gas and let your studded tires do the work."

The seven racers on the river skimmed the ice with ease. Lightning couldn't believe how fast he was going.

"This must be what flying feels like!" he said, relishing a blast of cold wind against his face.

Back on the main road, Shu, Nigel Gearsley, Rip, Miguel Camino, and Carla were regretting their decision. They were at a standstill on a bridge as they waited for a snowplow to clear the road.

Just then they heard a voice from the river below. It was Vitaly. "Hello, comrades! Everything okay up there?" he called.

The cars on the bridge sighed heavily.

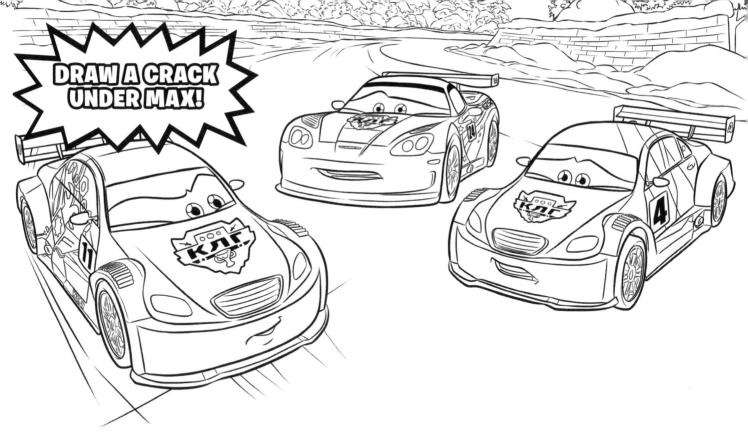

Down below, the river racers were facing problems of their own. Max's tire had cracked through the ice!

"Keep going without me," said Max.

"No! Never leave a comrade behind. There's more to this race than just winning," Vitaly said.

Jeff Gorvette drove up. "Let me stay with Max. You need to guide the others down the river."

Vitaly agreed and thanked Jeff. Then he called out to the others, "Stay the course! Onward toward the Hybridrome!"

Even though the river route was longer than the road course, the river racers were the first to arrive at the Hybridrome! As they began their laps around the stadium, several racing fans showed up to cheer them on.

Shu, Nigel, Miguel, Carla, and Rip zoomed into the Hybridrome and were shocked to discover that their fellow racers had already completed their first lap.

ADD LIGHTNING MCQUEEN!

"It looks like we have some catching up to do!" said Shu,
revving his engine and kicking up snow with his tires.

"Yes! This race isn't over yet!" exclaimed Miguel.

The cars entered the final lap of the race. Francesco and Lightning were battling for the lead.

Once, twice, three times around the track the racers went. Lightning and Francesco hurtled toward the finish line.

At the last second, Raoul slipped between the fierce competitors. With inches to spare, he edge out Lightning and Francesco for the win!

Vitaly was proud.

HOW DOES THE STORY END?
WRITE YOUR OWN ENDING.

_____

_____

_____

_____

_____

**It was a dark** and stormy night. The explorer
Charles Muntz had gone to bed, but his faithful pack of
dogs was still awake. Suddenly, a large flash of lightning
lit up the sky.

"Oh! That was very bright," Dug said.

Across the room, Alpha, Beta, and Gamma huddled together.
The three dogs hated storms, but they would never admit it.

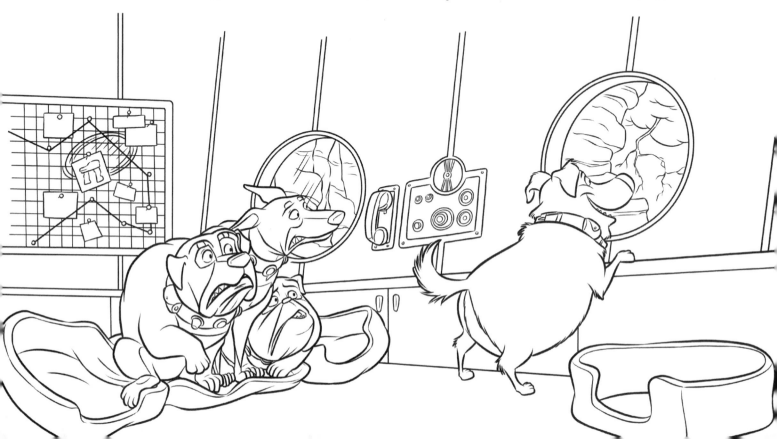

Just then, a loud rumble of thunder shook the airship. Beta and Gamma jumped. Beside them, Alpha cringed.

"Why isn't Dug scared?" Gamma whispered.

Alpha looked over at the golden retriever. "He's not smart enough to be scared," he said.

"Hey, Dug! Why aren't you scared of the storm?!" Beta called.

Dug turned. "Should I be scared?" he asked. "Maybe I am! Thank you, my pack. You are helping me be a better Dug!"

Alpha smiled slyly. He was always looking for ways to get Dug into trouble.

"You seem to be enjoying the storm," Alpha told Dug. "That must mean you are a *very* brave dog."

"I am?" Dug said. "You are Alpha and very smart. I will agree with you!"

"It's good that you are brave," Alpha continued. "Master told us that you should go outside to look for the bird. He thinks it might come out in this weather."

Charles Muntz had been searching for a special creature for as long as Dug could remember.

**ADD ALPHA TO THE SCENE!**

Dug's eyes lit up. "Master has thought about me? And has given me a *mission*? I must leave at once!"

Gamma and Beta started laughing. "There's no way Dug won't be scared once he's outside in that storm!" Gamma said.

"Master will be so angry when he finds Dug gone!" Beta added.

"Alpha, this is your best idea yet," Gamma said. "I don't want to miss watching him get scared! Let's follow him!"

Dug bolted outside, eager to start his mission. Within seconds, his fur was soaked by the pouring rain and ruffled by the fierce wind.

"Find the bird. Master has given me a job to do."

Dug was so focused on finding the creature that he didn't notice Alpha, Beta, and Gamma trailing behind him.

DRAW THE RAIN!

At the edge of the jungle, Dug paused. The trees cast long shadows and hid the moon and stars from sight. Dug kept going. "The dark is very quiet," he said.

Suddenly, Dug heard a rustling coming from the trees. Looking up, he saw countless pairs of giant glowing eyes watching him.

Far behind Dug, Alpha, Beta, and Gamma saw the glowing eyes, too. *"Aaah!"* the three screamed. "WHAT ARE THOSE SCARY EYES?!"

Dug moved around to the moonlit side of the tree. Looking up, he saw that the eyes belonged to a group of fruit bats!

"Hello!" Dug said. "You are not the bird. You are bats! You must be able to see very far from up there. Have you seen the bird?"

Alpha breathed a sigh of relief. "They're just fruit bats," he said. He was glad the eyes didn't belong to anything *really* scary.

But then Alpha scowled. He had expected Dug to be scared, but instead the golden retriever seemed *happy*!

DRAW MORE BATS!

The rain was still pouring down, but Dug didn't mind. Wishing the bats well, he continued on his way.

Dug had not gone far when he felt something small and slimy brush past his leg. "Something is on the ground near my leg," Dug said. "I wonder what it could be."

Behind Dug, Beta jumped into the air as something slimy bumped against his legs, too. "Snake!" he cried. "It's going to get me!"

"Shhh!" Alpha whispered. "Quiet! What is the *matter* with you?!"

Just then, lightning flashed and Dug saw that he was standing beside a rushing creek. A family of frogs was happily jumping past him toward the slick rocks.

"Hello! You are frogs," Dug said. "You are splashing about. You look like you are having fun. I am having fun, too. I am looking for the bird. Perhaps you have seen it?"

But the frogs just kept hopping along.

DRAW FROGS ON THE LOG!

As Dug walked deeper into the jungle, he heard leaves rustle on the path ahead of him.

"SQUIRREL!" Dug cried, turning toward the sound.

Dug looked around, but he didn't see anything. "I was mistaken. There is nothing there," he said.

**ADD DUG!**

Putting his nose to the ground, Dug continued on. Soon he came to a big clearing. On the far side, he thought he saw a tall, thin shadow moving in the darkness at the mouth of a cave.

Dug bounded across the clearing to investigate, wagging his tail eagerly. "Find the bird! Find the bird! Find the bird. . . ."

Behind him, Alpha, Gamma, and Beta crept toward the edge of the clearing. They were cold, tired, and frustrated.

"Great idea, Alpha," Beta complained. "We've spent the whole night roaming around the jungle getting soaked, and the only one who's been scared was Gamma, by a bunch of harmless fruit bats!"

"No I wasn't!" Gamma replied. "Besides, *you* were scared of a bunch of tiny frogs!"

"You are *both* scaredy dogs!" Alpha hissed at them. "There is nothing to be scared of. . . . Wait! Look!" The dogs turned in time to see Dug enter the dark cave.

"Dug is sure to be scared in there!" Beta said. "Or lost for good!"

52

Suddenly, a huge bolt of lightning flashed across the sky, illuminating the clearing. Through the rain, the dogs saw a horrible, fearsome-looking shadow standing at the mouth of the cave!

"Ahhhh!" Alpha shouted. "It's a monster! Run for your life!"

Alpha, Beta, and Gamma turned on their heels and dashed through the jungle, back toward the safety of the blimp.

Alpha's screams got Dug's attention. "Oh, it is my pack!" he said. "They must have been worried about me. They know how important my mission is and came to help. They are the best friends a Dug could ever have."

Dug tilted his head to one side. "I wonder where they are going."

From the mouth of the cave, Dug saw that the rain had slowed and the sun was rising. Its rays broke through the rain clouds, creating a breathtaking rainbow.

"The sun is rising!" Dug said. "That is why they are running! Master will be awake soon! I must go back and report."

DRAW
DUG'S BED!

"Beta! Gamma! Alpha!" Dug shouted when he got home.
Looking around the airship, Dug saw that the rest of his pack was
not there. "My pack must still be outside. I will wait for them."

Just then, Muntz walked into the room.

"Master!" Dug said. "I must tell you all about my mission!"

"What mission?" Muntz asked. "What are you talking about?
And where are the rest of dogs?"

Dug smiled at his master. "They are outside!"

"What?!" Muntz shouted. "They went out in *that* weather? *Ooooh,* they *know* how much I hate the smell of wet dog. They are in so much trouble when they get back. I swear . . . !"

Muntz shook his head and looked down at Dug. "Come on," he said, "I'll deal with those silly dogs later. Bet you they got themselves—"

ADD DUG'S MASTER, MUNTZ!

"*LOST!* We're *lost*!" Gamma cried.

The dogs were cold, wet, and terrified. And to make matters worse, the rain had washed away their footprints! They had no idea how to get home!

**HOW DOES THE STORY END? WRITE YOUR OWN ENDING.**

_____

_____

_____

_____

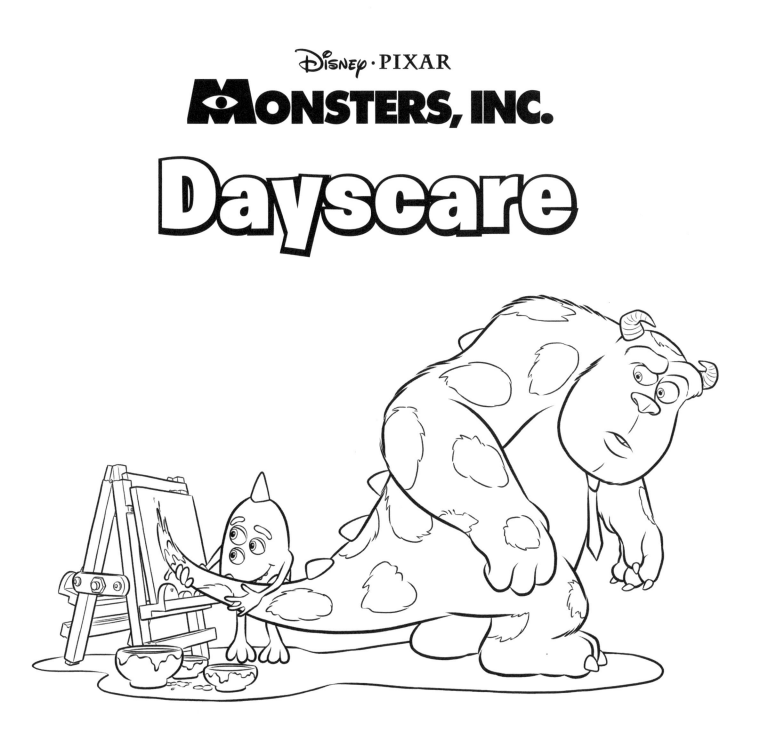

"**G**ood morning, President Sullivan," Celia said as Sulley walked through the front doors of Monsters, Inc.

"Good morning, Celia," he said with a wave. "You know you don't need to call me that."

Celia giggled. She was just teasing him.

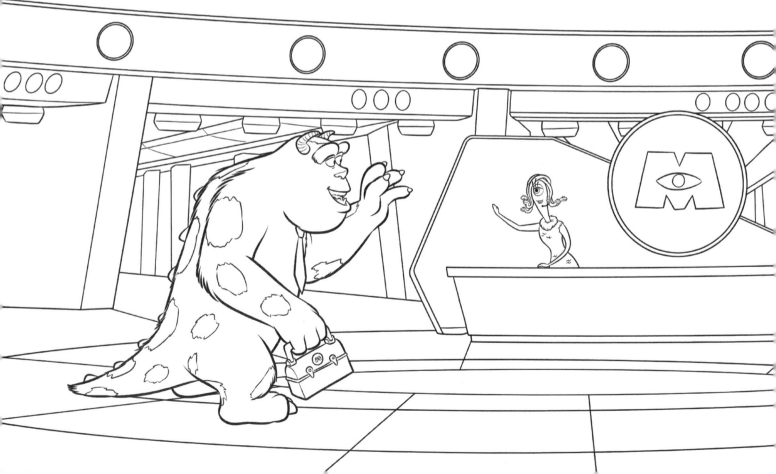

Sulley had just settled in behind his desk when his assistant buzzed him.

"Good morning, President Sullivan," he said. "Your ten o'clock joke brainstorming meeting has been pushed back to eleven. The Canister Safety Committee will now meet at nine thirty. And your weekly laugh training seminar will be at two o'clock."

"Thank you," Sulley said, sighing. He loved his new job, but sometimes there were just too many boring meetings!

Just then, his phone rang. It was the head of Monster Resources. "I'm sorry, President Sullivan," she said, "but both daycare teachers are out today with Swampy Pox!"

*Hmmm*, Sulley thought, *it must be fun teaching all those little monsters*. Suddenly, he had an idea—a crazy idea.

"Clear my schedule!" he called to his assistant. "I'll take care of this," he said into the phone. He headed to the Laugh Floor to find Mike.

"Sulley!" Mike said happily when he saw his friend. "Guess who just filled his daily laugh quota?"

"Perfect!" Sulley smiled. "That means you can teach daycare with me today!"

Mike's eye grew wide. "Um . . . laughs are one thing. I'm not sure about teaching an entire class of little monsters. . . ."

But Sulley grabbed his best friend and dragged him to the daycare room.

We SHARE
Because We CARE

DRAW SOME MORE
BABY MONSTERS!

The head of Monster Resources looked very pleased to see them.

"Look, everyone!" she cried. "It's your substitute daycare teachers, Mr. James P. Sullivan and Mr. Mike Wazowski! Guys, meet Fungus Jr., Patrick, Martha, Pearl, Gretel, and Randall's nephew, Rex."

She smiled. "See ya!" Then she ran out the door.

"Cute kids," said Sulley.  He wondered why the head of Monster Resources was in such a rush. "She must have a meeting to get to," he said. "Well, no meetings for me—today is all about fun!"

"Hello, everyone!" Sulley said to the class. "We're going to have such a good time today—"

In the middle of his speech, all the little monsters jumped up and started going wild.

"Ouch!" said Mike as he got hit with a stuffed monster. He shook his head at Sulley. "Fun, huh?" he said sarcastically. "Well, what are we supposed to do now, Mr. President?"

"Um . . . play a game?" Sulley suggested.

"Kids, who wants to play hide-and-seek?" Mike said.

"Ahhhh!" the kids screamed and ran off to hide. Mike covered his eye and began to count. "Ready or not, here I come!"

One by one, Mike and Sulley found the kids. Then Sulley quickly counted them. "Um, Mike, I think we're missing one," he said.

"You're right," said Mike. "Randall's nephew, Rex."

"And you'll never find him," Gretel added.

"This is why our teachers never let us play hide-and-seek anymore," Fungus Jr. said.

Mike gulped. "Sulley, I don't like this one bit!"

Just then Sulley had an idea. "It's too bad we can't find Rex," he said loudly. "Because it's snack time!"

"Here I am!" said Rex, suddenly reappearing behind Mike.

"We want snacks! We want snacks!" the kids screamed.

Mike ran to the cupboard and began handing out treats he thought the kids would like—gummy bugs, rotten apples, and mud-covered sardines.

Sulley smiled. "See, Mike, all we needed to do was—"

DRAW THE FOOD IN THE FOOD FIGHT!

"FOOD FIGHT!" the kids yelled. Instantly, food started flying across the room. Gummy bugs stuck to the walls and Sulley's fur. Mike got splattered with a some mud-covered sardines.

Little Martha crawled under the snack table and watched as she munched on a rotten apple.

"What a mess!" Mike moaned. Once he and Sulley had gotten the place cleaned up, they looked at each other. What should they do next?

"Let's try toy time," Sulley suggested.

Though it seemed like a good idea at first, it didn't last long.

"Mine!" Martha screeched.

"No, mine!" Pearl wailed.

Mike and Sulley tried everything to calm down the kids. They found toys in the closet. They played more games. But they just couldn't get the kids to settle down.

"Tie my shoes, Mike Wazowski!" Fungus Jr. demanded.

Mike rolled his eye. "You have got to be kidding me. A little help here!" he cried to Sulley.

"Right back at ya!" Sulley called back.

The day kept getting worse. Finger painting was a catastrophe. So were jump rope and dress up.

"Is this day over yet?" asked Mike.

Sulley checked the clock. "Not even close," he said.

"This is a total disaster," Mike groaned.

"There's got to be something we haven't tried," replied Sulley.

"You know, I just don't think so," Mike said, frustrated. "I think we've literally tried everything!"

"I'm sure there must be something . . ." said Sulley.

"I'm sure there must be something." Mike imitated Sulley's voice, acting like a kid.

"Don't be mean," Sulley said.

"Don't be mean." Mike imitated him again.

"No, Mike—look!" Sulley pointed to the monster kids, who sat on the floor, quietly watching them.

DRAW MORE BABY MONSTERS ON THE MATS!

The kids burst into applause.

"Again! Again!" Pearl cried. "We like your play!"

Now that they had the kids' attention, Mike and Sulley realized what they should do: put on a puppet show!

Mike told tons of jokes. And Sulley did lots of scary voices. The kids laughed and laughed. They had lunch, then took a long nap.

Finally, it was time for all the little monsters to go home.

Once everyone had been picked up, the two friends looked at each other and chuckled. Mike was covered with paint, and Sulley had a lollipop stuck to his fur.

"That was the toughest day I think I've ever had," Sulley said with a loud yawn. "I guess it's time to go home."

Mike eyed the pile of nap rugs in the corner. "Hey, let's rest for a minute before we head home," he suggested.

"Good idea," Sulley replied. "Hey, these are pretty comfortable!"

The next morning, Patrick was the first student to arrive.

"Oh, look!" Patrick's mom said to him. "Mr. Sullivan and Mr. Wazowski are already here."

Mike and Sulley sat up groggily.

HOW DOES THE STORY END?
WRITE YOUR OWN ENDING.

_____

_____

_____

_____

**N**emo was enjoying the perfect afternoon. He was playing tag with his octopus friend, Pearl. The two friends chased each other from sponge bed to sponge bed.

"Tag, you're it!" Pearl giggled as she tapped Nemo on the back with one of her eight tiny tentacles. "Bet you can't catch me!"

"We'll see about that!" Nemo said as Pearl jetted away, kicking up a large cloud of sand.

Nemo flipped his fins faster and chased Pearl past the edge of the sponge beds. He was just about to tag her when he spotted something tall and wide up ahead.

"What *is* that?" he shouted, pointing a fin over Pearl's head.

"What's *what*?" Pearl asked.

"Come on," Nemo said. "Let's go check it out!"

Nemo swam toward the looming object. It seemed to wave at them in the gentle current.

"W-wait for me!" Pearl called out.

Getting closer, Nemo let out an excited yelp. It was a huge seaweed bed! The bed was a giant maze of green and red seaweed. Some spots were almost too dense to swim through, while others formed small pockets of open space. Pearl and Nemo had never seen it before!

"This looks like the perfect hide-and-seek spot!" Nemo said to Pearl. "Want to play?"

Pearl looked around nervously. The sea had started to turn dark. "I would love to, Nemo, but I think we should head home. It's getting late, and both our dads will be wondering where we are."

Looking around, Nemo realized Pearl was right. It was time to go home for the night.

ADD PEARL TO THE SCENE!

DRAW CORAL AND SEAWEED!

When Nemo got back to his sea anemone, his father was waiting. Together they had dinner, and Nemo told him all about his afternoon with Pearl and the seaweed bed.

"That sounds like a neat place," Marlin told his son. "But now it's time for bed."

"Aww, come on, Dad," Nemo protested. "Can't I just stay up a little bit longer?"

Marlin shook his head. "Try to get some sleep, son."

Nemo settled into bed and closed his eyes. He told himself a long bedtime story. He thought about boring things, like math class. He even counted dolphins. But he still wasn't sleepy.

Finally, Nemo got up and swam to his father. "Dad, I can't fall asleep. I've tried, but I just can't. So I was thinking . . ."

Marlin looked up at his son. "Thinking, you say," he replied, trying not to smile. He had a pretty good idea what his son had been thinking. "What exactly were you thinking, son?" he asked.

"I think you and I should go to the seaweed bed now. That way you'll know it's safe, and I can go there tomorrow and play. I promise, when we get back, I'll go right to bed. Please?" Nemo begged.

Marlin looked at his son's hopeful face. Seeing the seaweed bed for himself *did* seem like a good idea. "All right," he said finally. "Let's go take a look at this new find of yours."

"Yes!" Nemo shouted, flipping over in excitement. "Let's go!"

As Marlin and Nemo swam through the reef, Nemo realized he was glad to have his father with him. Everything seemed scarier in the dark.

Squinting, Nemo looked for the seaweed bed. But in the dark, it was nearly impossible to see anything.

"Son," Marlin began, "are you sure the bed is out this far?"

Nemo nodded. "It is! I know it is! I just wish we could see a little bit better!"

Nemo was about to give up when he saw a light in the distance. The speck drew closer and closer, growing brighter and brighter, until it lit up the water all around Nemo. In the middle of the light was the strangest fish Nemo had ever seen.

The new fish had giant lights under her eyes.

"Hi. I'm . . . I'm Nemo," Nemo stammered, amazed.

"Hi!" the other fish said in a friendly singsong. "I'm Lumen."

"It's nice to meet you, Lumen," Marlin said. "I'm Nemo's dad.

How come we've never seen you before?"

Lumen fluttered around, causing her light to waver and flicker. "My family and I are nocturnal," she said. "We swim and play at night while everyone else is sleeping."

"Dad and I are being nightturnal, too!" Nemo said. "We're looking for this big seaweed bed I found this afternoon. Do you know where it is?"

"You bet I do!" Lumen said. "That's where I live. Follow me!"

Lumen led Nemo and Marlin to the seaweed bed. "Do you want to play a game?" she asked.

"Yeah!" Nemo shouted. "Can we, Dad? Please?"

Marlin nodded. "Just stay out here in the open," he said. "I'm going to go have a look around."

While the kids played, Marlin explored the seaweed bed to make sure it was safe. Behind him, he could hear his son counting to one hundred.

"Don't peek!" Marlin heard Lumen shout as she swam off to find a good hiding place.

ADD MARLIN!

Marlin pushed through the maze of thick green and red strands, swimming farther and farther into the seaweed bed. Suddenly, he realized how dark and quiet it had become. He could no longer hear Nemo or see Lumen's light!

Marlin spun around. He had no idea where he was! All he could see was seaweed. He was lost!

"Nemo!" he shouted. "Nemo! Where are you?"

But there was no answer.

Flipping his fins, Marlin tried to find his way out.

Just when he was beginning to think he would be stuck in the seaweed bed forever, Marlin spotted a faint light in the distance. "Nemo!" he called, swimming toward it. "Is that you?"

Following the light, Marlin made his way through the seaweed. The strands grew farther apart until finally he hit the open water. There, right where he'd left them, were Nemo and Lumen.

Marlin let out a sigh of relief.

"Dad!" Nemo said excitedly. "There you are! We didn't know where you'd gone! Don't you know better than to go swimming off by yourself in the dark?"

Marlin smiled. "I guess I should have followed my own advice!"

**HOW DOES THE STORY END?
WRITE YOUR OWN ENDING.**

_____

_____

_____

_____

_____

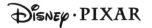

# THE INCREDIBLES

# A Super Summer Barbecue

**O**ne hot summer afternoon, Helen Parr stood in the kitchen frosting a chocolate cake. Her daughter, Violet, lay on the couch reading a magazine. Jack-Jack, the baby, sat in his high chair eating.

"Dash!" Helen called to her other son. "It's almost time to leave for the barbecue."

"Hey, Mom," Dash complained, running into the room at Super speed, "why do we have to go to some silly neighborhood barbecue?"

"Dashiell Robert Parr," Helen began sternly, "we're lucky to have been invited. It's our first neighborhood party. You know we're doing our best to fit in here. And remember: *no* Super powers outside the house."

"Right, Mom. No Super powers. The barbecue should be *loads* of fun," Dash said, rolling his eyes.

Just then, Jack-Jack threw a bowl of mashed peas. In a flash, Helen stretched her arm across the kitchen and caught the bowl in midair. Helen's Super powers as Elastigirl could come in pretty handy around the house, but she knew if her family's powers were ever discovered, they would have to move again.

Bob Parr walked in through the front door. "Honey, I've got the lawn looking shipshape," he said as he flexed his muscles. Bob used to fight crime on a daily basis as the Super, Mr. Incredible, but now his biggest weekend battle was the crabgrass. He sighed. "I finally got the last of that giant tree stump. If I could have used my Super strength, I would've been done three hours ago."

"You're right, dear," Helen answered, giving him a kiss on the cheek. "But you know we have to do our best to behave like a normal family. I only have a few more boxes to unpack, and I don't want to move this family again."

"No one will ever believe Violet is normal," Dash said.

Violet jumped up. "You be quiet!" she shouted. Then she threw a force field in Dash's path, knocking him to the ground.

"Kids, kids! That's enough. Let's get ready to go," Helen said.

A while later, the Parrs walked around the block to their first neighborhood barbecue. Helen smiled at Jack-Jack, who was in a baby backpack. "I hope they like my cake," she said as she walked to the dessert table.

Bob headed over to the grill to help out. Violet looked around for someone to talk to.

Dash watched some kids compete in a sack race. He couldn't race, because it might reveal his Super speed.

Then a boy walked up to Dash. "Are you too chicken to play? *Bawk-bawk-bawk*," clucked the boy, flapping his arms. Some of the other kids laughed.

Dash scowled. *If only I could race, I'd show that kid.* When the mean boy hopped by, he mysteriously tripped and fell.

"Weird," the boy said. "It felt like someone tripped me."

Dash smiled to himself and brushed off his sneaker. His speed had come in handy, after all. Luckily, his mom hadn't seen him.

Meanwhile, Helen was getting to know some other mothers and toddlers. She listened carefully as another woman talked about removing grass stains. When the woman began to discuss needlepoint, Helen realized that Jack-Jack had crawled away.

Out of the corner of her eye, Helen saw Jack-Jack atop a high brick wall. He was about to topple off!

In a flash, Helen shot her arm all the way across the yard and caught him. She sighed with relief and hugged Jack-Jack close to her. The other mother just rubbed her eyes and mumbled something about not sleeping much the night before. *Oops*, Helen thought.

Over by the grill, the men talked about the previous night's baseball game. When the steak was ready, Bob stepped forward.

"Allow me," he said, as he picked up a knife. *This steak is a bit tough,* he thought. *I'll just cut a little harder.*

*Craaack!* All of a sudden, the table splintered in two. The meat went flying and landed in the dirt. *Guess I used a little too much Super strength,* Bob thought.

"They just don't make tables like they used to, do they fellas?" Bob asked, as the others laughed politely.

103

Violet hadn't found anyone her age, so she sat under a shady tree and began to read. Then an old lady came over. Violet stood up to introduce herself. Once she did, the woman wouldn't stop talking. She told Violet about her miniature duck collection, her dentures, and even her hot-water bottle.

Finally, Violet couldn't stand it anymore. As the woman reached step thirty-three of her potato salad recipe, Violet pointed at something.

The woman turned, and Violet seized the moment. She jumped behind a tall plant and used her Super powers to make herself invisible. Even though only her body disappeared, the colors of her clothes blended in with the bushes.

Minutes went by. Finally, the lady noticed that Violet wasn't standing next to her. She looked all around and then walked away. When the coast was clear, Violet reappeared. She smiled to herself as she sat back down and opened her book.

Since the steak had fallen on the ground, Bob and the other guys decided to grill some hot dogs and hamburgers. Bob didn't help cook this time, but he did eat one or two more hot dogs than he should have.

Helen couldn't have been more pleased to see the neighbors enjoying her chocolate cake. Someone even asked for the recipe. She looked around the yard and spotted Dash telling a story. Violet was eating an ice cream cone with a girl her age.

*Wow, it looks like we really fit in here,* Helen thought as Bob walked over to her. He was finishing another hot dog.

Just then, she overheard one of the neighbors. "There's something strange about those Parrs," he said.

Helen grabbed Bob's arm. Bob looked at her. Had someone discovered them? Were their Super powers about to be revealed?

"Yeah, you should see how Bob mangled the table—and the steak!" a second neighbor said.

"Grandma said that Violet acted like she'd never heard of potato salad," a third neighbor chimed in. "And my son said Dash just *watched* the other kids race."

"All that may be true," someone else added, "but that Helen sure makes a terrific chocolate cake!" Everyone agreed, and the conversation ended.

The Parrs sighed with relief and chuckled to themselves. Their cover wasn't blown after all!

Maybe they were a little strange compared to the average family, but they were doing their best to act normal. Bob and Helen rounded up their kids and headed for home, pleased with the way things had gone.

"I think we could really like this neighborhood, Bob," said Helen as they reached their house. Then she gave him a great big kiss, which the kids did their best to ignore.

"I think you're right," answered Bob. "I've got a good feeling about things this time."

"Sweetie, would you mind moving the car over a bit?" asked Helen. "I need to get out of the garage to go grocery shopping tomorrow morning."

"Sure thing, honey," Bob replied. "I'll be right in."

Bob looked at the car sitting in the driveway. The street was quiet. *It's too easy,* he thought. Besides, a guy's gotta work out every now and then. Bob picked up the car, balanced it on one finger and put it down on the other side of the driveway.

HOW DOES THE STORY END? WRITE YOUR OWN ENDING.

_____

_____

_____

_____

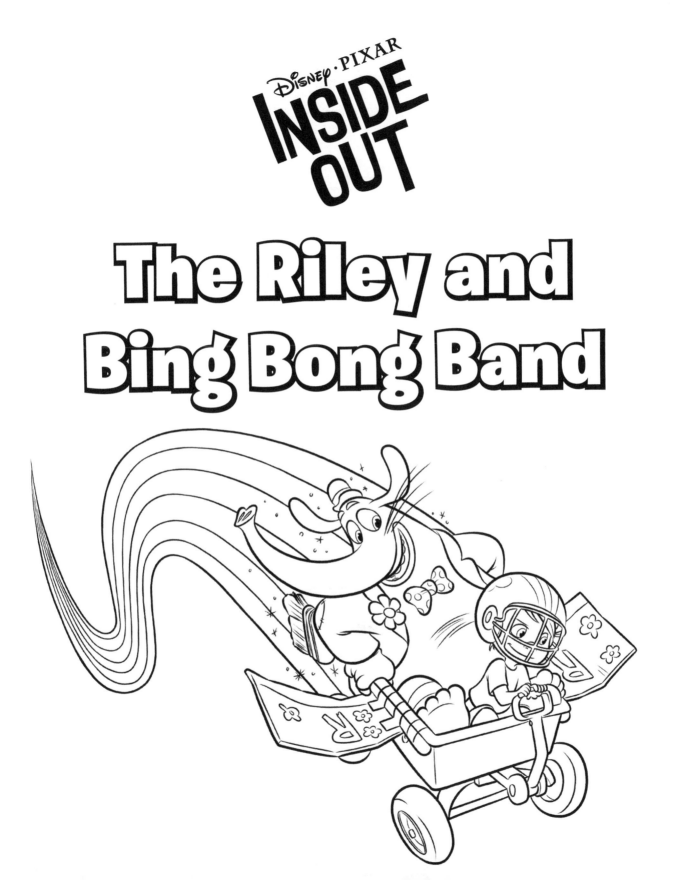

**R**iley and her imaginary friend Bing Bong loved making music together. One day, after playing some new songs, Riley turned to Bing Bong. "We should go on tour!" she said.

Bing Bong smiled. "Great idea! Let's go to Australia in our rocket! We can play for the kangaroos!"

"Woo-hoo!" Joy exclaimed. "A new adventure!"

But Riley's other Emotions weren't as excited as Joy. "Australia is awfully far away," Sadness said. "We'll get homesick."

Fear looked up from his pile of papers on Australia. "There's koalas, wallabies . . . Wait. What's a platypus? It has poison in its feet!"

"Poisonous feet?" Disgust said. "I can't, I just can't."

"Look at this!" Anger said, pointing to a picture of two kangaroos boxing. "Do they really box? I'm starting to like this plan!"

"We're going to Australia!" Riley announced to her mom and dad as she ran through the kitchen.

"Be back for dinner," Mom said. "I'm making my famous mashed potatoes."

"And don't forget, there's a big ocean between Minnesota and Australia," Dad added.

"We'd better bring our floaties," Riley whispered to Bing Bong as they ran upstairs to Riley's room.

ADD
BING BONG!

"It's a GIGANTIC ocean!" Fear screamed as he and the other Emotions looked at a map.

"Awesome!" Joy said.

"Yeah, great. Salty hair and humidity . . ." Disgust said.

"Ohhh," Sadness groaned. "This isn't a good idea. What if we get lost out there?"

"We could always become pirates!" Anger suggested.

When Riley and Bing Bong had all their supplies, they climbed into the rocket.

Riley turned to Bing Bong. "Ready to check all systems?"

"Check, check, and . . . check!" Bing Bong said, pointing to the controls.

"Activating rocket booster. Mission Control, all systems are go!" Riley shouted. Together, Riley and Bing Bong began to count down. "Five, four, three, two, one . . . BLASTOFF!"

But nothing happened! Riley and Bing Bong looked at each other, confused. Then Riley smiled. "Of course! The rocket can't fly without fuel!" she said.

Together, Riley and Bing Bong began to sing their special song. "Who's your friend who likes to play?" The rocket answered back, binging and bonging. Then it rumbled and roared as it flew out of the window!

The Emotions watched as Minnesota disappeared into the distance. "Good-bye, home," Sadness said.

As they soared over the ocean, Riley and Bing Bong saw a shark, a sea turtle, a walrus, and penguins! So far, this was the best trip ever. Excited, they started talking about all the things they would see in Australia.

"Dad said koala bears eat gum trees. Do you think they can blow bubbles?" Riley said.

"Of course!" Bing Bong replied.

Just then, Bing Bong noticed that the water was getting closer. "Are we landing?" he asked. Suddenly, the rocket fell toward the ocean!

"*AHHHHH!*" Riley and Bing Bong screamed as they plummeted. Riley grabbed the radio. "Mission Control, we have a problem!"

"We're done for!" Fear shouted, stuffing his head inside a paper bag.

"I knew it," Sadness said.

"The fuel! We were so busy being excited, we forgot to sing!" Joy said. Quickly, she plugged in an idea bulb.

"We have to sing!" Riley shouted.

"I'm so scared! I can't remember the words!" Bing Bong screamed.

Riley shouted the words to the song as the rocket sputtered. Bing Bong joined her, and the two sang louder and faster than ever before.

"Who's your friend who likes to play? Bing Bong, Bing Bong! His rocket makes you yell hooray!"

The rocket lifted back into the air!

DRAW THE CONSOLE BUTTONS!

Soon they could see land. "Australia!" Riley shouted.

The Emotions also cheered. "We made it?" Fear asked, stunned.

The creatures in Australia welcomed Riley and Bing Bong with big smiles.

"Play us a tune, mates," a koala said.

Riley and Bing Bong looked at each other. Grinning, they picked up their instruments and began to play. They played all their songs, and the crowd went wild.

Suddenly, a familiar smell drifted through the air.

"Mom's famous mashed potatoes," Riley whispered to Bing Bong. "It's time to go home."

Together, they said good-bye to their new friends and rocketed back to Minnesota.

"So . . . how was Australia?" Dad asked Riley as she pulled along the wagon.

HOW DOES THE STORY END?
WRITE YOUR OWN ENDING.

_____

_____

_____

_____